The
Princess
and
the Prick
the

The
Princess
and the Prick

Walburga Appleseed

Illustrated by
Seobhan Hope

HQ
An imprint of HarperCollinsPublishers Ltd
1 London Bridge Street
London SE1 9GF

This edition 2020

2
First published in Great Britain by
HQ, an imprint of HarperCollinsPublishers Ltd 2020

ISBN: 978-0-00-840110-8

Page design and typesetting by Emily Voller

Printed and bound in Great Britain by Bell and Bain Ltd, Glasgow

MIX
Paper from
responsible sources
FSC
www.fsc.org
FSC® C007454

This book is produced from independently certified FSC™ paper
to ensure responsible forest management.

For more information visit: www.harpercollins.co.uk/green

To Ian, my favourite feminist

An Easy Recipe For a Girl

Mix sugar with spice and nice things.*
Stir gently or else she might break.
Enjoy your girl!

*Be careful not to spice her up too
much, or you'll end up with a tart.*

An Easy Recipe For a Boy

Snip off a good-sized dog's tail.
Mix with snips and snails.
Stir.*
Enjoy your boy!

*Be careful to stir vigorously, or else
he might not become a real man.*

Fairy
Tales

Sleeping Beauty

'May I kiss you?' he asked.

She didn't answer. She was asleep.

So he kissed her anyway.

Snow White

'I'll buy the dead girl in the
see-through coffin,' he said.

'You can have her for free,'
said the dwarves.

And the deal was sealed.

Cinderella

The prince would never have
recognized her,
If it wasn't for her feet.

Hansel and Gretel

Gingerbread by gingerbread
they ate up her house.

When there was nothing left,
they slung her into the fire.

And lived happily ever after.

The Princess and the Pea

'I didn't sleep well,' said the princess.
'My back was achy and uncomfortable.'

'It was the pea, it's proof she's a
real princess,' rejoiced the prince.

I had my period, thought the princess.
But she never said.

Goose Girl

'Your new wife's not the princess, she's
the servant,' said the dead horse's head.

The prince knew he could
trust a dead horse's head.

So he killed his wife.

Little Red Riding Hood

'Come undress, jump into bed with me,
let me devour you,' said the wolf
to Little Red Riding Hood.

'Deal,' she said.

The Frog Prince

'I will play with you, and eat with you, and sleep with you,' said the frog.

'Oh no,' said the princess.

'Oh yes,' said the frog.

And he did.

Rapunzel

'Rapunzel, Rapunzel, let down your hair,'
said the witch.

'Rapunzel, Rapunzel, let down your hair,'
said the prince.

'And how about your pants?'

Rumpelstiltskin

The king wanted to marry the
person who could spin gold.

Rumpelstiltskin could spin gold.

Gay marriage should have been an option,
But it wasn't.

21

Bluebeard

'Here's the key to my darkest secrets,'
said Bluebeard to his wives.
'But never use it. Or else.'

The wives used the key.

And else.

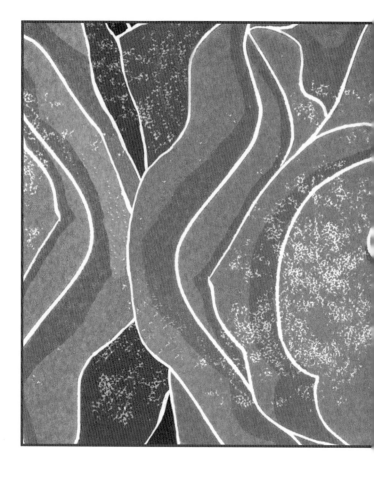

Thumbelina

She went through a lot of
abusive boyfriends.

Then married a fairy king with
a penchant for pink flowers.

Arabian Nights

'We make out, and then you tell me
another story. Or I slit your throat,'
the sultan said to Sheherazade.

Thus he lay the foundations
for a healthy relationship.

1001 nights later, they married.

The Twelve Dancing Princesses

The scruffy old soldier ratted on the princesses.

As a reward, he could choose which one to marry.

He chose the eldest, for she was closest to his age. A decent man.

Nursery
Rhymes

Jack and Jill

We'll never know what happened to Jill,
But we are glad that Jack was fine.

Georgie Porgie

Georgie Porgie didn't read the signs.

Polly Put the Kettle On

Polly's work is futile.

Little Miss Muffet

Miss Muffet is a wuss.

Goosey Goosey Gander

We'll never know what the man was doing in the lady's chamber.

We can only guess.

Mary Mary Quite Contrary

Mary has her own mind and
that is not a good thing.

Peter Peter Pumpkin Eater

If in doubt about one wife,
Maybe get another one.

Sing a Song of Sixpence

Queens aren't great with cash, but they do like bread and honey.

Cry Baby Bunting

Don't count on your mother for anything.

As I Was Going
to St. Ives

Kits, cats, sacks, wives are all the property of one man.

I Had a Little Hen

Who needs a housewife when
a chicken will do?

The Old Woman Who Lived in a Shoe

The old woman knew nothing of family planning, but she liked shoes.

Childhood
Films

Peter Pan

'A jealous female's all it took!'
Rejoiced a gleeful Captain Hook.

Lady and the Tramp

Though life on the streets is really tough,
the Lady likes her bit of rough.

Beauty and the Beast

'Just a bit of locking up
helped you fall in love.

And now we can be married,
like two turtle doves.'

The Jungle Book

An unnamed girl with curvy hips
who dreams to be his wife,

Leaves young Mowgli itching
for a quiet domestic life.

Aristocats

Cats can't help flaunting their gender.
Girl cats have waistlines so slender.

The Wizard of Oz

Four witches in the Land of Oz,
all experts at their job.

One phoney wizard rules them all,
and he's a shifty knob.

The Little Mermaid

Ain't she charming, how she
teeters on her aching feet?

Selling off her voice for love
is worth it, and so sweet!

The Lion King

Nala has abundant powers:
she's smart, and born to reign.

Good for her, to be allowed to
lick the new king's mane.

Bambi

To seduce your Bambi-boy for
woodland rumpy-pumpy,

Flutter those eyelashes, or
risk just looking frumpy.

Aladdin

A vile vizier, a useless dad,
or yet a pompous prick?

Just go and rub your own lamp,
then you'll never have to pick.

The Smurfs

Gargamel shapes Smurfette from clay,
to lead all the Smurf boys astray.

But wild black hair and rough
of voice simply will not do;

Better far a lush blonde mane
matched with a high-heeled shoe.

Children's Classics

Alice in Wonderland

In her dreams, Alice can do
all sorts of things.

Then she wakes up.

Tintin

Blistering Barnacles!
Where are all the bloody women?

Watership Down

Hazel, a gentle, compassionate buck,
Asks of the does he's captured:

'Are they a good fuck?'

The Wind in the Willows

'Hang it,' said Mole. 'Why are
there no girls around here?'

Little Women

Remain little, woman.

There's a dear.

The Lion, the Witch and the Wardrobe

'Nylons and lipstick will corrupt
your morals,' says Aslan,
a lion with a big mane.

Daughters of Eve, beware!

Asterix: The Women

Would you rather be
young, pretty and dim,

Or old, ugly, and still pretty dim?

The Hobbit

The road goes ever on and on.

But where are the lady travellers?

Heidi

Aunt Dete wanted to have
a life without children.

Will she ever hear the end of it?

The Famous Five

Julian and Dick: captains ahoy!
George is nearly as good as a boy.

Anne serves ginger beer with grace.
Isn't it spiffing that she knows her place?

Myths &
Legends

Adam and Eve

'She made me!' said Adam.

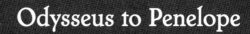

Odysseus to Penelope

'I'll be two weeks, max. Promise.'

Pandora's Box

A man would never have opened it.

Menelaos and Paris to Helen of Troy

'It's all your fault. You're just too passive-aggressively beautiful.'

Arthur to Guinevere

'Let me show you my Excalibur.'

Zeus to Hera

'You're my wife, eternally.
How does that not make you happy?'

Theseus to Ariadne

'I'm just not that into you.'

Penelope and her 108 suitors

Think of all the fun she could have had.

Oedipus and his Mum

Moving swiftly on...

And they all lived
happily ever after.